...IPPA GERRETT AND INTREPID TEACHERS EVERYWHERE! J.J.

FOR KIT. L.C.

www.juliajarman.com
www.lynnechapman.co.uk

Class Three All at Sea
by Julia Jarman and Lynne Chapman

First published in 2008 by Hodder Children's Books
First published in paperback in 2009

Hodder Children's Books
338 Euston Road
London NW1 3BH

Hodder Children's Books Australia
Level 17/207 Kent Street
Sydney NSW 2000

A catalogue record of this book is
available from the British Library.

ISBN: 978 0 340 94466 0
10 9 8 7 6 5 4 3 2

Printed in China

Hodder Children's Books
is a division of Hachette
Children's Books.
An Hachette Livre UK Company.

www.hachettelivre.co.uk

Class Three
ALL AT SEA

JULIA JARMAN

Illustrated by

LYNNE CHAPMAN

Hodder Children's Books

A division of Hachette Children's Books

On the day Class Three went to sea,
they saw donkeys dancing on the quay.

They saw some sea lions
skimming stones.

Sunny Days
BOAT TOURS

But they didn't see...

...the **skull** and **cross-bones**.

They heard
Teacher say,
'Wear a life jacket,'
'Listen to me!'
and 'Stop that racket!'

Sunny Days
BOAT TOUR

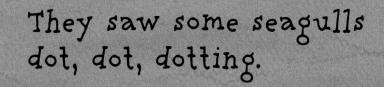

They saw some seagulls
dot, dot, dotting.

But they didn't hear...

...the pirates plotting.

They saw some dolphins near the shore,
doing sums, '2 and 2 make 4.'

They saw two pelicans sniff and sneer.

But they didn't see pirates...

...getting near.

They saw an octopus tied in knots
and they untied him. 'Thanks a lot!'

They saw fishes flying in the sky, as Octopus waved,

'Goodbye! Goodbye!'

But they didn't see...

...**Hairy-Legs** board the ship.

They didn't see him grab Phillip.

They didn't see
Pirate Bogey-Nose

grab Jackie,
James and
Jenny-Rose.

They didn't see **Pirate Fish-Breath Frank**
make poor Lenny walk the plank.

Or the chief called **Rotten Teeth**
grab the captain, whose name was Keith.

'See that island up ahead?
Sail straight to it, or Class Three's dead!'

The chief had a map with
a spot marked 'X'.
Percy saw it
with his specs!

Treasure Island.

Class Three's teacher didn't see.
She was perched on
a pirate's knee.

But...

...little Lenny, swimming the crawl,

hailed a porpoise,
playing ball.

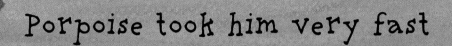

Porpoise took him very fast

to Octopus
who was aghast.

'Quick!' he cried to his big brother.
'One good turn deserves another.'

But time, alas, was running
out for **Rotten Teeth**,
the smelly lout,
yelled...

'I AM GETTING VERY CROSS!'
as the captain stuttered, 'I th-think we're lost.'

Then all of a sudden,
they heard a whoosh,
followed by
a mighty

sploosh!

As Octopus landed, then his brother,
they grabbed one pirate, then another.

'You'd better let go of Class Three,'
Lenny said, as **Rotten Teeth's**
eye popped out of his head.

Soon the trembling pirates fled the ship. All except for **Pirate Pip**.

'Miss and me, we'd like to marry.'

'Later,' said Pat and Pete and Harry,
for they'd seen something
by the light of the moon...

Treasure Island!
'Not a moment too soon.'

And Harry spied
the spot marked 'X'.
His telescope saw
every spec.

'Sail straight onwards, Captain Keith.
And try to miss that coral reef!'

Sailing fast, they reached
their goal where Class Three
dug a very deep hole.

And at the bottom – yes, you've guessed –

they found a stuffed-full treasure chest!

So if ever your class goes to sea,
remember what happened to Class Three.
And if pirates board, don't make a fuss...

just make friends
with an octopus!